THE SHEPHERDS' PRAYER

Richard M. Barry

Copyright © 2005 by Richard M Barry

Published by RM Barry Publications
Centennial, Colorado

RM Barry Publications
P.O. Box 3528
Littleton, CO 80161-3528

Website: www.shepherds-prayer.com

Printed in the United States of America

ISBN 0-9767290-4-0

Chapter One

Micah beamed with pride as his aged yet still clear hazel gray eyes looked upon the large family gathered at his table. They were a handsome lot. His sons had grown tall and strong. All but the youngest had taken wives, who were gathered with them along with Micah's many grandchildren. His youngest son John had now engaged to be married too. Micah had arranged the marriage for the sixteen-year old with a business associate of his, and the union of his son with the man's fourteen-year old daughter would enlarge the profits of both merchants. That left Anam as the only single man at the table, a realization that made him feel even more out of place than usual. He was nearly thirty now and he still had not married. He was not related to the others by blood, but he still considered them his brothers; yet this event again highlighted the sad fact that he simply did not fit in.

The eldest son, Aaron, turned to his white-bearded father and said, "Are you going to bestow a blessing upon the lad?" He then winked at his youngest brother and said, "After all, he is to be married, so he will need all of the help he can get!"

The brothers roared with laughter. Their wives rolled their eyes and smiled demurely, the way women were expected to. The children joined in on the laughter, though they didn't understand the joke. Anam didn't think it was very funny, but he loved hearing the laughter of children. They always seemed to have such light hearts that laughter came naturally for them. In a way he was envious of them.

Micah stood up from his position at the head of the table. His beloved wife Miriam had died a few years earlier, and he insisted that her seat next to his remain vacant as a permanent tribute and reminder of her life. His sons had urged him to remarry, but the old man had no interest in any other woman. The patriarch fixed his gaze upon his family, and then raised his eyes toward heaven. "We beseech ye, oh Yahweh, maker of heaven and earth, to bestow thy blessings upon this child John. Bless the union he will enter into with the fruit of children and the goodness of heaven."

They all bowed their heads and recited a solemn "Amen" in perfect unison.

The women then went to work at once, carrying heaping platters of food to the large wooden table. Micah had ordered the fatted calf slaughtered, and they feasted on it along with lamb meat, fresh vegetables and wine.

Anam was pleased that John would now be married and start a family. He wished him nothing but happiness. But his mood was morose as he ate quietly and kept to himself, in stark contrast to the others. The brothers, as always, were their boisterous selves. Jacob, the second oldest brother, finished his third glass of wine and poured himself another. His wife whispered something to him. Jacob shook his head dismissively, then turned toward Anam and said, "You are the luckiest amongst us, my good man."

Confused, Anam quietly said, "How do you mean?"

A red-faced Jacob said, "You have no wife nagging you telling you how much to drink!"

He slapped Anam on the back and all of his brothers laughed. "I'll drink to that," Aaron said.

From across the table, Micah locked eyes with his adopted son. The old man's deep wrinkles around his eyes spoke volumes. He felt Anam's pain, but would not embarrass him by addressing it here at the table. Anam caught the look on his compassionate father's face, and it helped him to get through the rest of the dinner without punching one of his brothers. They had no idea that their good-natured barbs were so hurtful.

After dinner, Anam slipped away from the family and went out into the fields. The sun was setting behind some hills in the distance. The temperature was dropping and he pulled his cloak up more tightly around his neck. "You are the living God," he said aloud into the gathering darkness. "I need guidance. This cannot be my lot for the rest of my life. There must be more. Please show me."

He stood and listened to the wind as it softly fluttered

amongst the trees. A faint whisper came to his ear. Whether or not it was audible, he could not tell. Yet it was a voice…and it told him the time had come at last to go to Micah, his father, and pour out his heart.

Chapter Two

The night wore on and the festivities died down. The children fell asleep first, followed soon by their fathers (helped by too much wine) who were dutifully joined by their wives. As Micah was a successful merchant, his home, though not ostentatious, had room enough for his married sons and their families when they would visit.

Anam, however, had no intention of going to sleep yet. He felt the hand of God upon his shoulder, urging him to go forward and speak with his father openly. Man to man. There was no turning back now. Anam gathered up his courage and went back inside the house. The sweet aroma of the evening's feast still lingered in the air as he quietly made his way to his father's private quarters, careful not to wake any of his kin.

A faint light flickered from beneath the closed door. *He must be up reading, it is best not to disturb him,* Anam told himself. He turned to walk away, but then something stopped him. *No, I must do this,* he resolved.

The young man knocked on the door lightly.

There was the shuffling of footsteps, and Micah appeared in the doorway. "Anam," he said, "I thought you were asleep like the others."

"I could not sleep, Father."

Micah ushered him inside and closed the door. "Now," he said, "tell me what is bothering you."

How does he know something is bothering me? It must show on my face. I swear that man can see right through me sometimes! Anam's eyes turned toward the large parchment scrolls carefully laid out on the table next to Micah's bed, illuminated by a dim lantern. "I see that you were reading from the Sacred Scriptures, Father. I am sorry for disturbing you."

The old man smiled and rested his weary bones in a chair next to his bed. "To tell you the truth, I needed the break. What I was reading was, well, let's say, very disturbing."

Though he wanted to get right to his question, Micah's words were riveting to the young man and he wanted to know more. "Is it from the Pentateuch?" he asked, referring to the portion of Holy Writ he was most familiar with.

"No, it is from the inspired utterances of the Prophet Isaiah."

Anam nodded when he heard the name. He was certainly familiar with the great Prophet, but embarrassed to admit he did not know all of his writings. "He was a great man of God who lived hundreds of years ago, is that not correct?"

The old man nodded his head. "Yes, but his words seem to speak just as clearly to our own day. The passage I just read tells of a mysterious figure. A servant who comes and gives his life to save his people."

Anam vaguely recalled hearing of this particular poem once before, but he wanted to know more. "How can a servant save anyone?" he asked, perplexed.

"I do not know, my son. But Isaiah says that this servant, when he comes, will be despised by men, reviled. He will suffer much, but his suffering will not be in vain. In fact, through his suffering God will heal the nations, and this suffering servant will be glorified."

"The Prophet has indeed given us a strange story, father," said Anam, "but what does it mean?"

Micah sighed deeply. "I wish I had the answer. I don't fully understand it myself, but I think what he is trying to tell us is that we must look at suffering in a different way; we must see it from God's perspective rather than just man's. This was written in the distant past, but even today our people suffer greatly, under the oppression of the Romans. It makes me wonder if he was speaking to those of us alive today."

There was silence for a moment as Anam absorbed his words.

Micah leaned over and patted the young man on the shoulder. "But I know you did not come here to discuss prophecy," he said. "So tell me, what is on your mind?"

Anam cleared his throat. "Please understand that I mean no disrespect by this question. You have been a kind and loving father to me all of my life, and I thank God every day for you. But…"

Micah's old eyes looked upon him with compassion. "But you want to know about the circumstances of your birth. You want to know where you came from."

Bowing his head, Anam quietly replied, "Yes."

"I knew this day would come," said Micah. "In fact, it is to your credit that it took so many years before you finally came to me and asked. You have always been a most respectful boy. Now I will tell you the story."

Anam felt his throat tighten as he sat and listened to the story he had always wanted to hear.

It was many years ago, I have lost count but I believe it was about thirty years. I was traveling alone, not a wise thing for a merchant to do but in my younger years I took chances. I was on my way home from a very successful trading mission in Jerusalem. It was late in the day and I was tired, as was my donkey, which was heavily laden with merchandise I had purchased in the great city. I was filled with happy thoughts of returning home, where I knew my beloved wife Miriam would be waiting for me. I also anticipated the money I could make with all of the fine products I had shrewdly negotiated for.

But then, before me on the road, I came across a sight that would change my life forever. There was a ditch off to the side of the road. I thought I heard something, a wailing sort of sound, and I stopped dead in my tracks. My donkey began braying and kicking. Something had frightened him. The first thought that crossed my mind was that there were thieves lying in wait. They would pounce upon me and steal my goods. In fear of my life, I unsheathed my dagger and moved cautiously toward the edge of the ditch to take a closer look.

I cannot tell you how astonished I was when, rather than bandits, I saw a Roman horse toppled over on its side. It was dead, after having apparently been ridden to exhaustion. But tied to the side of the animal, in a rugged sack, was an infant. The child was crying, and I picked him up in my arms to comfort him.

Anam had been listening intently. He swallowed hard as the reality of Micah's words sunk in. "It was me?"

"Yes."

"I was all alone?"

Micah gently stroked his long, white beard, a gesture Anam knew he did when something was bothering him, and continued.

There was a woman. She was pinned beneath the dead horse. With all my strength I somehow managed to pull her out from under the carcass. But I was too late. She too was dead. That woman, I can only presume, must have been your mother.

A single tear appeared in Anam's eye as he waited for the old man to continue.

I do not know what her name was, but I gently lay her body across my donkey, leaving most of my merchandise by the side of the road, and took her back to our town for a proper burial.

Of course, I took the baby with me too, carrying him…I mean, you, with me in my arms the remainder of the trip.

Ah, you were a fine looking child, Anam, and once I held you, your crying stopped. I wanted to consider you as my own child from that very first day, as did Miriam when I showed you to her. However, when we took you to the elders at the synagogue, they noted that you had already been circumcised. According to the laws of our people, given to us by the Most High, that meant you were a Jew and had already been given a name on the day of your circumcision. It would dishonor your parents, alive or dead, to give you another name. That is why we deemed it necessary to call you "Anam," which literally means, "no name." It fulfilled the letter of the law.

The elders told me that my solemn duty at that point was to try to find your family and return you to them. But the circumstances of your birth were shrouded in mystery. The only clue that I had, in fact, was the lambskin blanket that you had been wrapped in when I found you.

Anam cocked his head. "How could a blanket tell you anything about who I was?"

Micah nodded as if to confirm a long-held belief. "The time has come for you to see as well as to hear."

The old man ambled over to an oblong wooden chest that lay at the foot of his bed. Ever since he was a child, Anam had wondered what was inside, but his father always kept it under lock and key. The aged hinges groaned in protest as Micah opened the lid and the musty smell of things stored away for many years permeated the room. He carefully retrieved a lambskin blanket from deep within the chest and handed it to Anam.

"It is beautiful," he said, as his fingers lovingly caressed the soft, white wool.

"Go on," said Micah. "Read the inscription."

Embedded with ink into the tanned hide were these words, which Anam read aloud: "Glory to God in the highest heaven and peace on earth to men of good will, through Jesus Christ Who was born of Mary in a stable in Bethlehem and Who, wrapped in swaddling clothes, was in a manger, He Who is the Savior of the world."

Micah smiled. "Yes, yes. I remember those words, each and every one of them, as if I had just read them yesterday. They have remained with me, close to my heart, all of these many years, and I have often pondered their meaning."

Anam stood up, his eyes alive with wonder. "Father, I do not understand what these words mean. Who is this Jesus? And Mary? I do not know of these people. Are they my relatives?"

Micah shook his head. "I tried to find out the answers, boy, but it has remained a mystery to this day. I want you to know, however, that this blanket is rightfully your property. I have faithfully preserved it for you, for this very day, and now I want you to keep it."

Tears welled up in the young man's eyes as he hugged the blanket close to his body. It was a connection to his past, the only link, in fact, and it stirred within him a passion to know more.

"You said this blanket was your only clue, Father. Did it lead you any closer to the truth?"

Micah continued with his story...

The truth was indeed what I was seeking. With the blessing of our town's elders I set out back up the road the same way I had come, in hopes of finding your family. When I came to the town of Bethlehem, I heard of a terrible evil that had befallen that place. It seems that the king had received information that a child had been born who would someday present a challenge to his throne. So he ordered all of the male infants in that town to be slaughtered. The killing was horrific, the grief it caused, indescribable.

I surmised that your mother must have escaped the town to save you from a certain and cruel death. In her flight, she happened upon a horse that belonged to one of Herod's soldiers. Being terrified out of her senses, she urged the horse on as fast and as far as it would go, until it finally collapsed in the desert.

I thought perhaps this great tragedy would lead me to your family. My heart rejoiced in thinking how happy they would be to have you back.

But it was not to be. The more I asked about this mystery child that I had found, the more hostile the people became toward me. They were angry and suspicious of me. Soon, I was met with a wall of silence as one by one they refused to speak with me. Realizing the futility of my quest, I returned home. And from that day on, you became my son.

Hearing this story now for the first time, nearly three decades after it had occurred, all sorts of thoughts and emotions flooded Anam's very being. Micah's incredible tale had prompted more questions than answers. And who was this mysterious Jesus that the lambskin blanket spoke of? He was determined to find out.

"Father, I know what I must do. I shall travel to Bethlehem myself and seek out answers." He then bowed his head in deference to the kindly old man who loved him so much. "That is, sir, with your blessing."

"Come here," Micah said, gesturing Anam to his side. He put his hands on the youth's head and uttered a prayer over him. Anam closed his eyes as he listened intently to every word. Then Micah dismissed him and sent him on his way saying, "May the God of Abraham, Isaac and Jacob be with you, my son. And may the living God who alone guards all truth guide your every footstep."

Chapter Three

Anam had traveled before with his father Micah on many trading journeys. Once they had even sojourned as far north as the land of Lebanon. Ah, how he recalled the magnificent cedars, tall and majestic still, as in the days of old. But this trip was much different. It was not for commerce, or any sort of monetary gain. In fact, he felt almost like a beggar, as he carried with him only those meager provisions he could carry in a sack he had tied to the end of a thick stick with a leather thong.

Another major difference from his previous trips was that this time he was alone. This was by choice. He did not want a companion, as he considered this a personal quest—something that he needed to do all by himself. God would be with him, and that would be enough.

The road he chose to take was not well traveled, and this too he did with a purpose. Yes, it would be more dangerous than the more popular roads, with their merchant caravans, military patrols and everyday foot traffic, but that was fine by him. He needed time to think, and to pray. For as far back as Anam could remember these things always came to him more powerfully in solitude.

Though it was late in the year, the sun nonetheless beat down upon his face relentlessly throughout the midday hours, and he would occasionally wipe his brow with the sleeve of his tunic to keep the stinging perspiration out of his eyes. Later, as dusk approached, Anam picked up his pace and walked more briskly along the dirt path, hoping to reach the inn his father had told him about before the sun set behind the gently sloping hills in this distance.

He came to a bend in the road. Surely the inn must be up ahead. From the directions he had been given, he knew he was close. But as his eyes peered into the twilight, only more road lay ahead of him. That was okay; he simply returned his thoughts to where they had been all day. He kept asking God, what exactly was it that he was searching for? Is a name really all that important? Will it change who I truly am? Can I be a righteous man even without a heritage? As always happened when he became so deeply reflective, Anam found himself with more questions than answers.

As darkness continued to envelop the road, Anam realized that he would not reach the inn soon enough. Traveling on a dark road was not wise. Even though he carried few possessions, alone and unarmed he could easily fall prey to bandits who might just as well kill him for not providing anything for them to steal. So Anam took refuge in a farmer's field. There was a large, slightly bent willow tree commanding the far edge of the field. He placed his provisions on the ground, spread out a woolen blanket and lay down on his back to sleep. It was so quiet out here. Back home he could always hear his father's snoring, the neighbors arguing, or one of his brothers stumbling toward the outhouse in the middle of the night. There was none of that now. He was alone with his thoughts. Far above him, the vault of God's heaven presented itself to his eyes. Anam recalled the words of David: *The heavens declare the glory of God; and the firmament showeth His handiwork.* Yes, wise words indeed. He would keep them, along with the other sacred writings, close to his heart, just as his father had always instructed him. And without a doubt, the stars were so beautiful tonight, each one of them brightly shining against the backdrop of velvety blackness. Truly, what a magnificent display of Yahweh's power, he thought. This ruler of the universe, the One who spoke and all this creative wonder leapt into existence, why would He ever care about a humble man like me? A man without a name. Yet I know there is a place for me in this world, a purpose for my life. If only I can find it.

He fell asleep that night counting the multitude of stars, trying to comprehend so much that was beyond his reach.

The next morning, the crowing of a barnyard cock off in the distance awoke Anam from his slumber. He rubbed his eyes and laughed as he heard his stomach rumbling. How long had it been since he had last eaten? It had been almost a full day now, save for some biscuits he had taken with him and munched on during yesterday's walk. He stretched, gathered up his belongings, and made his way across the field and toward the road. How different everything looks in the daylight, he mused. It was the same field, but dappled in sunshine it seemed so much more pleasant. As fascinated as he was by the stars, Anam loved the morning. It was his favorite time of day and always gave him a renewed sense of what was possible.

As it turned out, within a mile the little-used road Anam had walked all day yesterday linked up with the much more busy road that headed directly into Bethlehem. A man with a donkey crossed his path. Anam said, "Peace, friend." The man just nodded and kept going. Anam waved to farmers he passed working their fields. They paid him little attention. He also saw women carrying water back to their families, but he knew better than to greet them. Conversing with women who were not kin or close acquaintances could be scandalous, and Anam wasn't looking for trouble. Just answers.

Finally, he entered the town of Bethlehem itself. It was much smaller than he had expected, basically just a few small shops such as a blacksmith, a livery stable, a tavern bar and an inn. With his stomach growling even more loudly, Anam decided to first stop at the tavern for some food. A young man greeted him when he walked through the door. The smell of freshly baked bread permeated the air. His mouth watering, Anam told the young man he would like to have some breakfast. "Sit down over there," the young man instructed, pointing to a small table and two chairs, "and I will bring you food."

Anam sat down and placed the sack with his belongings next to him on the floor. A few minutes later the young man brought him bread, water and some steamed vegetables. He placed the food on the table, along with two plates. "Do you mind if I join you?" he asked. "I haven't eaten yet myself."

With a warm smile, Anam said, "Please, friend, sit and eat. I could use the company." He extended his hand and said, "My name is Anam."

Shaking his hand briefly, the young man's eyes beheld that same questioning look people had always had when Anam revealed his very uncommon and somewhat mysterious name. He said, "I'm Saul. Do you have family here in Bethlehem?"

Anam carefully chewed his food and drank some water. He could feel his strength returning as the nourishment worked its way through his body. "Actually, the point of my visit is to find out about my family."

Saul lapsed silent as he waited to hear more.

Finished with his first piece of bread and starting his second, Anam explained his story, concluding by telling the young man about the inscription on the lambskin blanket. "In fact," he said with a smile, "I have it right here with me." He reached into the sack at his feet and with great care retrieved his treasured possession. "Read it for yourself, Saul. It is a fascinating riddle."

Saul got up and walked over to Anam's side of the table. He carefully studied the words inscribed upon the lambskin, and then took two steps backwards. "I think you better leave now," he said.

"What?" Anam was confused. "I haven't finished eating… and I still have to pay you. How much do I owe?"

His eyes cold, Saul said, "Nothing. I want nothing from you. Just leave this place now. Please."

Anam was shocked by the man's sudden change of heart. "Have I offended you in some way?" he asked.

The young man refused to answer. Anam left him some coins to pay for his meal, and went on his way, perplexed by this abrupt turn of events.

For the rest of the day, as he walked about the little town seeking answers, the hostility of the townspeople seemed to follow him wherever he would go. At first, when he would simply state that he was seeking information about his family, they would initially be friendly and helpful. But as soon as he would mention the inscription on the lambskin, they would turn their backs and walk away from him. Often cursing. One man even spat upon him. Anam's instinct was to punch the man in retaliation, but he restrained himself. A stranger in town—and one whom nobody seemed to like—he was obviously outnumbered and would surely end up on the losing side of any confrontation.

After a while he stopped mentioning the lambskin. Still, he made no progress. Nobody was forthcoming with any information that might help him find out about his parents and the circumstances of his birth. Dejected, Anam arrived at the inn at the center of town just as dusk was settling over the little hamlet. Tired from being on his feet all day, Anam was by this point just looking forward to a hot meal and a good night's rest.

The innkeeper was a short, plump old man. His name was Johanan. "Are you here for lodging, stranger?" he asked.

"Yes, my good man," Anam replied. "And a meal too, if you would be so kind. I have with me enough money to pay for both." He held out some gold coins his father had given to him.

Johanan's eyes beheld suspicion. Ignoring the glittering money, he asked, "What is your name?"

Returning the money to a pouch beneath his garment, Anam avoided direct eye contact. "I am called Anam," he said.

"Anam," said the innkeeper, wrinkling his nose. "What a strange name. Tell me, young man, who is your father? And from whence do you come?"

These were the same questions he had been answering for the townspeople all day. And each time, his honest reply, along with his own request for information, was met with nothing but contempt. There was no reason to believe things would be any different with this elderly gentleman, but Anam was committed to remaining honest. "My father is Micah, he is a prosperous merchant, and our home is many miles to the south of here."

Johanan scratched his head as his eyes carefully scrutinized Anam's face. "There is something familiar about you," he said thoughtfully. "It is as if I have seen you before. Tell me, have you accompanied your father here on business perhaps?"

"Yes, sir," he replied. "But we never spent any time here in Bethlehem. We only passed through town."

"Yet, somehow, your face reminds me of a man I once knew."

Now Anam's curiosity was running rampant. It could not be Micah whom he resembled, for he was not his "real" father, at least not in the biological sense. Was the innkeeper remembering the man from whose seed he was conceived? Anam decided this was a good opportunity to break the ice regarding the purpose of his visit. "Sir, may we sit down?" he asked.

The old man smiled. "Yes. In fact, you came just in time for the evening meal. My wife is ill and will not be joining me at my table tonight. Come, let us sit and eat together."

Two servants brought them their food in the dimly lit dining room. There was roasted lamb along with bread, fresh made butter and goat cheese. After bowing their heads in prayer, they began eating. The innkeeper took a sip of his wine and said, "Now, where were we? Oh yes, you were going to tell me why you are here."

Anam swallowed a piece of meat. It tasted wonderful as it satiated his hunger. He cleared his throat and began. "I think I know, perhaps, why I look familiar to you."

Johanan sipped more wine as he patiently waited for him to continue. He was one of those people who seemed to have all the time in the world and would never be in a hurry.

"My father Micah is a good and kind man. However, he and I do not share the same lineage. My 'real' parents, I believe, are from here in Bethlehem." He then went on to explain the story that Micah had told to him of how he had found him on the roadside, along with the dead woman who most likely had been his mother. He also showed him the lambskin with the inscription. This man had seemed friendlier than the others, so perhaps his reaction would be different. But as soon as he read the inscription, his face looked as if had seen a ghost, and he averted his eyes.

Anam quickly put the lambskin away and tried to salvage their conversation, though he feared he would now once again be rebuffed. "So," Anam concluded, "maybe the reason I look familiar to you is because you may have known the man who was my father by blood. Please, sir, I beseech you, do you recall his name?"

"I'm afraid my memory is not as sharp as it was in my younger years," said Johanan. "Maybe my mind is just playing tricks on me."

Anam noticed a drastic change in the old man's demeanor after he'd related his story. And especially after he had shown him the lambskin. It was as if now he wanted nothing to do with this newcomer. But Anam was determined not to give up so easily. He had come too far. Looking

Johanan straight in the eyes, he asked, "Please tell me more. As an elder of this town I am sure you know the circumstances of what happened here those many years ago back when I was born."

Johanan finished his wine and ordered a servant to bring him some more. The pleasant mood between the two men had turned stone cold and silence reigned between them until Johanan's second glass of wine arrived. He drank some, put down the glass and said, "Listen, I should not even be sharing such evil with you, but against my better judgment, I will."

"Evil?" Anam was dumfounded.

"Yes, young man. Evil. That inscription brings back terrible memories of an awful time. A great period of violence and suffering that tore at the very heart of our peaceful little village."

Anam swallowed hard.

Johanan seemed as if he were immersed in his own memories, relating the tale as if he were reliving all of it right before his eyes. "That one of whom the inscription speaks, all of the killing was because of him!"

"Do you mean..." Anam's voice was creaking and his throat became dry..."Jesus?"

The old man glared at him. "Do not utter that name in my presence!" he thundered. "I should have my servants throw you out into the night!"

"Sir, I'm sorry," he apologized. "I meant no offense."

There was an awkward, strained silence for a dozen heartbeats. The servants out in the kitchen were trying to keep busy, pretending they could not hear what was being said.

"Well…anyway," grumbled the innkeeper as he finished his second glass of wine and ordered a third. "The last time I heard anyone using that name was many, many years ago. It was those foolish shepherds with their tall tales that led to the soldiers coming here, and with them such wanton bloodshed and death."

"Please tell me more. Who were these shepherds? What did they do to provoke the soldiers? Were they criminals?"

Johanan shook his head. "Not in the strict sense of the word, I suppose. But what they provoked was worse than anything I've ever seen by any evildoer. Even a thief at least has a purpose for the bad deeds that he does. These fools, on the other hand, had no reason for spreading their vile delusions. No reason, that is, other than the corruption of their own drunken minds."

This last comment, thought Anam, sounded a bit ironic as the old man was now well into his third glass of wine. But he implored him to continue; he was spellbound by what he was hearing.

"In fact, it was right around this time of the year, as I recall. These shepherds came into town with a fantastic story. All made the same claim. They said that they were visited by an angel."

Anam's eyes widened. "An angel?"

Johanan finished his glass of wine. "Ha! Is that not the height of foolishness? Why would an angel of the Most High visit such lowly men? Tell me, would you not think, if he were to send a messenger, would it not be to the important men? Those with power? Imagine, they actually expected us to believe their ridiculous story."

With a shrug, Anam only said, "My father has always told me that the Lord works in mysterious ways. Maybe He had a special reason for the angelic visit."

The innkeeper shook his head. "Wait, young man. You will not want to defend these bad men and make excuses for them after you hear the rest of the story. They stormed into town telling every man they could find that a heavenly host had come here to announce the birth of the Messiah. Right here in Bethlehem!"

The food on Anam's plate remained almost untouched. He was fascinated by the old man's tale and could no longer focus on eating. What could all of this have to do with the circumstances of his own birth, and what befell his parents?

"Nobody believed them. They tried to support their claim by pointing out the presence of three powerful and mysterious men, astronomers from far off countries, who visited our area a short time after the child was born. But most everyone in town believes that was just a coincidence… especially after what happened next."

His tone of voice now carried with it even stronger bitterness.

"Is what happened next the reason you say these men were doers of evil, and not just harmless drunkards?"

Johanan nodded his head vigorously. "Yes indeed, young man, that is correct. By saying that the Messiah had come, they provoked the wrath of Herod, who became jealous and determined to stop what he saw as a threat to his own power. Resolved to kill this newborn future king, he ordered his soldiers to murder every male infant child in our precious town. The slaughter...the slaughter of those innocent babies was like an onslaught from the very depths of hell. They came, and..."

The old man's eyes were filling with tears, and though he tried to continue, too choked up with emotion, he could not.

Anam felt awful for dredging up such terrible memories for this man. Yet, he had one more question that he needed answered, and even though he wanted to cause no further hurt to the innkeeper, he asked nonetheless. "My good sir, I beg you, please tell me, does that inscription that I had shown you somehow bear witness to these horrific events?"

Johanan's eyes shifted from sadness to anger. "Without a doubt," he said. "The name on that lambskin of yours...you know the one."

Tentatively, in a quiet voice Anam muttered, "Jesus?" knowing how much the man across the table from him hated that name.

An angry nod confirmed it.

"The shepherds said that this...Jesus, was the promised Messiah?"

"Yes! And that is why all of the killing happened," said Johanan, rubbing his eyes. "Now, I have told you enough. You may have a room for the night if you wish. No more of this talk about bad things. It is all in the past and we cannot change what has happened."

What a frustrating way to end their conversation. Anam still had so many more questions. Especially about this Jesus. He now more than ever had to find out all that he could about this man, and why his very birth had caused such a tumult. Then a thought came to him. The shepherds! He would confront them and find out the truth. He asked the innkeeper where he might find them.

Johanan sighed deeply. "In fact, I happen to know that they return to this area, to the outskirts of town, this time every year. But, my friend, as I have told you, they are bad men. If you are a righteous man, you will want nothing to do with them."

"I do not fear them," he boldly declared. Actually, that was not entirely true. He was more than a little worried to face these rough herdsmen who were responsible for so much killing, not to mention his own unfortunate circumstances. Yet, something deep down inside of him compelled him forward.

Reluctantly, the innkeeper provided him with the information he sought. He gave directions to where Anam would find the shepherds camped out at their winter feeding grounds.

Anam thanked the old man and retired to his room for the night. In silent prayer he implored God for His guidance and protection. Tomorrow promised to bring him the answers he had asked himself his entire life. He felt as if he had just made a date with his own destiny.

Chapter Four

The winter feeding grounds, according to the innkeeper's directions, were only a few miles outside of town. Anam awoke with the sun, feeling as if he hadn't slept at all. In fact, he knew he did not get nearly the rest that he had needed. He had spent the night wrestling with his coverings, hoping for some steady sleep. But it only came in fits and starts as he kept wondering what it would be like when he found these men. Would his courage fail him at the critical moment? Would he turn and run rather than confront them with the questions that he was burning to ask?

As he got dressed, visions of what it must have been like in the last days of life for his mother kept haunting him. She must have sacrificed her own life in order to save him, her son. What bravery…and how unnecessary. These foolish men and their tall tales were the cause of it all. What would he say to them? If they knew he was there to accuse them of complicity in his mother's death, they would be unlikely to surrender much information. He tried to think of a plan, but nothing came to him. Finally, deciding to play it one step at a time, he paid the innkeeper and set off down the road again.

31

The road veered off outside of Bethlehem and led into a vacant, hilly land without another soul to be seen. The sun was climbing in the eastern sky, yet there was still a slight chill to the air this early in the morning, especially when the breeze would kick up. With each passing step Anam knew he was drawing closer to them, and he could feel his heart rate slowly ramping up. *It must just be these steep hills,* he kept trying to convince himself. Yet he knew it was more than that. The fear of the unknown gripped him and would not let go. Still, he trudged forward, expecting to see something around each beckoning curve. But all there was for the eye to see were barren pastures and still more hills. The road had now become just a rough trail, with no markings to distinguish it. It was filled with rocks and he had to be careful not to twist his ankle on any of them.

After an hour of walking, he grew a bit hungry. He had been so eager to get going that morning that he had skipped breakfast, simply paying what he owed to the innkeeper and leaving in haste. Anam found a large boulder and sat down upon it, placing his sack of belongings next to him. He breathed in the cool, clear air and held it in his lungs for a moment. It felt good as he slowly exhaled. He was thinking of eating some of the biscuits he had brought with him when suddenly he thought he heard something. Cupping his ear with his hand, he strained to hear more clearly. Sheep! Unmistakably, that is what he heard, there were sheep bleating off in the distance.

Well, he thought, there was no turning back now. The winter pasture must be close by, probably right over the next hill. He forgot all about his hunger, gathered up his provisions and set off at a run toward the hill, stopping, out of breath, as he nearly crested it. He was not ready to make his appearance just yet, nor did he want to see them. First he needed to gain control of his breathing, and slow down his racing heart. Letting them see him like this would betray a sign of weakness, which was the last thing he wanted to do.

He found a scrubby little patch of bushes, and, sitting on the ground beneath their meager shade he closed his eyes and sought God. *I have come this far,* he said to his unseen Creator, *please do not let me fail now. Please, Lord, it has been so many years now, let me find the courage to learn the truth. I want to move on with my life, but that will never happen if I do not go through with this. I beg of you, God, make Your strength my strength, and I will not fear these harsh men, nor turn away from them. Thank you, Lord. Amen.*

Without further hesitation, Anam got on his feet and made his way the remaining twenty feet to the top of the hill. The wind was blowing his hair as he scanned the vast area before him. Off to his right he could hear the sheep more loudly now. He could see them calmly grazing in the late morning sun. But still no shepherds. Where were they? He began walking down the back side of the hill, his eyes scouring the land for any sign of them.

At the bottom of the hill he thought he smelled smoke,

and his heart quickened because he knew they were not very far away. He crept through some bushes, and the group of men clustered around a campfire spotted him at the same moment that he first saw them. There were five of them, sitting in a semi-circle around the fire. "It looks like we have a visitor," said one of the younger shepherds.

Anam stepped out of the bushes, determined not to let them see how nervous he was.

"Come and share some breakfast with us, friend," said one of the older ones, a thin man with a thick gray beard.

Anam approached them cautiously. "My name is Anam," he said. He waited, expecting them to greet his name with the same unfriendly curiosity he'd grown accustomed to. Surprisingly, they didn't. In fact, it didn't seem to mean anything to them. They just smiled.

He walked over to the little group and sat down with them. "My name is Eli," said the oldest of them, whom Anam surmised was their leader. Another man came over and handed him a cup of sheep's milk and some cheese, which he gladly accepted. Eli then introduced the other shepherds. "There are still others amongst our group," he said, "but they have not yet arrived."

Anam remembered what the innkeeper had told him about the shepherds returning to this same place every year. He decided to jump right in with a question and to forego the small talk. "Oh," he said, "so you mean all of you come from afar? You do not live here?"

He sipped his milk, his eyes examining the small band of men over the rim of his cup. Some of them, especially the younger ones, seemed a bit fidgety and nervous, as if they did not like being asked questions such as this. It clearly made them uncomfortable.

The young shepherd who had first spotted him spoke up. His name was Jonas. "Perhaps we should be the one to question you," he said, his voice edgier than before. "Who are you, and why have you come here to our camp?"

Anam had been prepared to ask questions, not answer them. Then again, he was guilty of nothing, so why, he finally said to himself, should he be afraid to reply. "I live many miles from here," he declared. He looked at the group and could tell they were waiting for him to continue, so he did. "But I have good reason to believe that I may have been born in this very area."

More than a few eyebrows were raised. One of the shepherds, a large man with big hands, asked in a surprisingly calm, non-threatening voice, "Does your family hail from Bethlehem?"

Anam replied, "I cannot say for sure. In fact, that is why I am here. I have been told that you men might know about my family."

Jonas, the youngest of the group, was still looking at him suspiciously, but the short, nearly bald man named Samuel said, "We are but humble shepherds, Anam, but we will help if we can."

Before Anam could speak, Jonas piped up. "Who told you we could help? The people of that town have never shown anything but hatred toward us. Tell me, why should we help you?"

Anam glared at the young man. If they are all like him, he thought, it's easy to see how the townspeople dislike them so.

"Please excuse our young friend," said Eli, putting down his bowl and looking upon Anam with compassion in his eyes. "He had a most unfortunate encounter with some of the people of Bethlehem when he arrived here a few days ago. I am afraid it has put him in the wrong frame of mind. I assure you he means you no offense."

"None taken," said Anam, realizing he may have been too hasty in judgment. He looked over at Jonas, and the young man seemed to soften a bit.

"Actually," said Eli, "you have come here at the right time. This is our winter pasture. We, a group of old friends, meet in this very place for a very specific purpose at this time each year. I am sure that amongst our number, somebody will be able to help you. There was a time, when I was younger, that we shepherds knew everyone in Bethlehem, and we were well regarded." Eli let out a deep sigh as he stared thoughtfully into the fire. Then he looked at Anam again. "That was long ago. But still, it's quite possible one of us may have known your relatives."

Anam finished his milk and put the cup down. Without

being asked, Samuel rushed over and refilled it for him from his flask. "Thank you," Anam said quietly. He wanted to delve right into asking about his family. After all, they were showing kindness toward him. But then it occurred to him that it would probably be best to further befriend them first, before getting into any topics that might cause strife. He asked what he thought was a very simple question. "So, why do you gather here at this particular time of the year? Does it have something to do with caring for the sheep?"

They all smiled at one another, as if sharing information they alone were privileged to know. "It's not easy to explain," answered Eli. "But tonight our brethren from neighboring territories will be joining us. Please come as our guest." He smiled at Anam, before adding, "And then you will learn everything."

Anam spent the day in solitude. He did not want to be with the shepherds until later that night, though they said he was welcome to make himself at home at their camp while they waited for their friends to arrive. Instead, he wandered the meadows in the surrounding countryside, lost in his own thoughts. The sun was shining pleasantly by the latter part of the afternoon, so Anam found a log and sat down to rest. He took some small loaves Samuel had given him out of his pack and ate one of them. It was quite good. He laughed to himself as he thought, *well, at least I will never starve as long as I am out here with these fellows.* He was truly impressed by their hospitality. Did the people in town realize how gentle and harmless these men really were?

An eagle soared overhead in the nearly cloudless sky. The proud creature, he thought, brought glory to God by its power and grace. Yes, even the animals had their own special place in creation. Unlike him. In moments of quiet like this, Anam felt more alone and out of place than ever. While his brothers were enjoying their lives and siring offspring to make their father Micah proud, here he was off in the middle of nowhere trying to learn about his own birth. Sometimes he even felt cursed. But whenever such a thought would grip him, he would quickly dismiss it. To think that way would be to dishonor God, and that was something he would never do. "I will find out Your plan for me, Lord," he murmured into the wind. "In Your own good time."

As the sun sank low in the west, Anam knew that soon he would meet with the shepherds again. This time there would be more of them, as they would be joined by the rest of their group.

He got up and began walking. For a while, his thoughts were happy. Things were turning out better than he could have hoped. These men were so cooperative, and maybe they would indeed be able to help him. But then doubts subtly crept into his consciousness. He really didn't know these men very well, having only met them a few hours earlier. Maybe these were just the good ones he had encountered. The evildoers might be those assembling just over that hill up ahead at this very moment. His father Micah had warned him that bad men always committed their unrighteous deeds at night, under the cloak of darkness. "They hate the light," the old man had warned him, "because the light reveals their sin."

Fear suddenly crept over him like an ill wind. *Maybe I should turn and leave,* he thought as he approached the top of the hill above their encampment. With the rapidly gathering darkness he began to struggle with his worries even more. *There are no civilized people for miles around. I could be killed out here and nobody would even know it. If I do not return, will Father come looking for me? What about my brothers? Do they really think of me as family enough to care about my fate? What if…*

"There you are!" a voice snapped him out of his thoughts.

It was Jonas, the youngest of the shepherds, standing directly in front of him. Anam felt as if his tongue cleaved to the roof of his mouth.

"Eli was worried about you," said Jonas, reaching his hand out to Anam's shoulder. "He sent me out to look for you. And to ask your forgiveness for my behavior this morning."

Relief swept over Anam's face as he realized the young man's sincerity. He smiled and said, "As I told you, I took no offense. It seems you have good reason to be wary of strangers."

As they walked together over the top of the hill and down the other side toward the clearing, they engaged in friendly conversation. "Truth be told," said Jonas, "I have never been a hateful kind of man. But it is hard to not feel bitter when others mean you harm simply for who you are."

Anam contemplated his words as they walked along in the cool air, the last rays of the sun swiftly disappearing behind even more hills in the distance. "These people in Bethlehem," he said, "I have heard about their hatred toward you, and I think I know the reason why." As soon as the words had left his mouth, he wished he hadn't uttered them. The last thing he wanted was to insult this youth now that he had befriended him.

But Jonas merely shook his head. "That is because they do not know the full story. They do not know the truth."

Anam was familiar with the allegations made against the shepherds, but he didn't push the subject. In any case, by this time they had arrived at the shepherds' campsite, which was now a very loud and crowded gathering of about twelve men.

Eli and Samuel greeted them warmly and introduced Anam to the newly arrived shepherds. After sharing a communal meal, at which Eli delivered one of the most beautiful prayers of thanks Anam had ever heard, they all sat around a roaring bonfire. Its heat felt good, and its light co-mingled with that of the full moon to turn the night into a pale reflection of the day.

One by one the more elderly of the shepherds began to speak. The reason for their gathering became immediately clear, and it was intricately linked to the story that Anam wanted to hear about—their tale of being visited by an angel and all that followed. It had happened at this very same time of the year, thirty years ago now. Ever since, they had all gathered together at this place each year during this same week to recall and celebrate what all of them ardently considered blessed events. One by one, they recounted their experiences. The last to speak was Eli, who, though a simple man, spoke in words of profound eloquence.

He began, "I will recall that holy night for as long as I live…"

Chapter Five

Eli tells his story...

I was much younger back then, of course, and I required very little sleep, so I was happy to accept the duty of keeping watch at night. It was cold and clear, just as it is this very evening. I pulled my cloak up around me and walked about the meadow. Unlike myself, the sheep within my charge lay fast asleep. As I watched the gentle creatures in their peaceful slumber I always wondered, do these animals have dreams the way men do? I laughed, thinking that all a sheep would probably dream about would be greener pastures. But I, as a young man, indeed had dreams—many of them. I envisioned myself traveling to far off lands, doing exciting things and going on one adventure after another. Yet, I knew nothing remarkable was likely to happen in my life. As a shepherd, as my father before me and his father before him, my life was to be what it was—a simple existence, tending to the sheep day in and day out and not much more.

I was ruminating on these things while lazily staring at the clear night sky. There were so many stars out that night, more than a man could ever count. To pass the time I began connecting the stars to one another with imaginary lines in my mind. Some became great sailing ships, others were lions or bears. If I really stretched my imagination I could even build mighty fortresses and glorious palaces. A few of these shiny points of lights came together to form sheep. Ah yes, always back to the sheep...

Anam noticed the men around the fire all smiled and nodded in agreement. One of them took a large piece of wood and tossed it on the fire. The orange flames crackled and radiated a warm glow that felt good to Anam, since the air had turned cold with the darkness. Eli continued...

But then, something happened, a brightening of the sky that startled me. At first it seemed to me it was merely my eyes playing tricks on me. I had most likely gone far too long without sleep, and my weary mind was not serving me well. Yet, what I was seeing was no illusion. This was really happening! A powerful beam of light was descending from the heavens, bathing a spot behind a tree about a hundred feet away with its splendor, whiter than the snows of Mount Hermon.

I stood there frozen as stiff as a statue. My jaw hung open, my young eyes were wide with wonder. I did not understand exactly what was happening, but something deep down inside of me let me know that I was in the midst of a presence beyond the natural, and not of this earth. The light grew even more intense, flooding out the rays of the moon and the twinkling of the stars. My instincts suddenly took over, and I dropped my staff and dashed off to summon the others. Running as fast as I could, within moments I was back at the little shelter where we used to sleep. Out of breath, I called them out to see what was happening. Those who were still awake ran out immediately, as the others groggily rose from their slumber.

"What are you rambling about, boy?" one of the elders grumbled. "Listen, lad, is this your idea of a joke! I am telling you right now that…"

Before he could finish, another man interrupted. "Look!" he shouted.

The rest of the men all turned in stunned amazement. The light was now encompassing the entire area. There was no denying it. Some of them cowered in fear, others shielded their eyes with their hands and stared at this incredible sight.

"Come, follow me," I said, and off I ran. The others were right behind me. There were twelve of us. We stopped directly in front of the tree, now lit up brighter than noontime, yet with luminosity unlike the sun. It was the middle of the night, but we had to shield our eyes from the brightness. This was a heavenly light—that is the only way that I can describe it.

Someone declared, "I see a form like a body!"

"It is an angel!" I shouted, and I fell to my knees. All around me my brethren likewise dropped to the ground, the older men pushing their faces hard against the grass. There was much fear and trembling.

Anam turned his attention to the other shepherds around the fire as the flames cast a flickering glow across their faces. Only a few of the men there had been with Eli that fateful night, and it was easy to tell who they were.

Tears had begun to well up in their eyes, and some already had streams flowing down their cheeks. They seemed to be reliving the events of thirty years past as Eli continued...

We all knew instinctively that we were in the presence of a heavenly messenger. But why had he come here? To us, of all people! We were but lowly shepherds, men whom the world considered as nothing of much value. Was there sin in our lives? Had the Lord sent his angel to rebuke us? All of us were praying silently, hoping for mercy as we waited for whatever might happen next. I remember holding my breath for what seemed the longest of times.

Then we heard a voice. To my ears, it seemed to convey sweetness and authority in the same instant. It was the voice of a young man, but somehow unlike any I had ever heard. "Be not afraid," he said. "I bring to you tidings of great joy."

Up until that point, my eyes had been downcast toward the ground. I was afraid to gaze upon this powerful angel of the Lord. But the tone and quality of his voice was soothing, and removed all of my fear. Still on my knees, I lifted my eyes up toward him and beheld the splendor of his beauty. This angelic being had the form and the countenance of a man, but in a way far beyond the glory of an average man. It was the face of one whose dwelling place was in the heavens, far beyond the abode of mortal man. The expression upon that face reinforced his words. He was not here to condemn us at all. Quite to the contrary, he had appeared to us on that night to make a joyful announcement that would change our lives, and indeed the entire world.

The angel's wings were like those of a large white dove, only much brighter, and they were fluttering with a rhythmic grace that soothed my fear.

Eli paused for a moment and stirred the coals in the campfire until countless sparks rose into the darkness, disappearing in the star-filled night. As he did so, he said...

A steady stream of brightly glowing embers fell from his wings as they waved in the night sky. In his soft yet powerful voice, the angel proclaimed, "Today, in the City of David, the Savior has been born."

We were awestruck by his words. The Savior! This was too good to be true. All of Israel had awaited this day for so long, for eons before even our fathers' fathers were born.

As he spoke, the angel seemed to become even brighter, which I would not have thought possible. I could hear the joy in his voice, and I understood that he took great pleasure in delivering this magnificent news to us. I then heard him say, "The Savior Who is Christ. Christ the Lord."

At the mention of that name, the angel's voice became rich with adoration. He crossed his wings and bowed his head in a sign of utmost reverence. Then he spoke to us again: "This shall be a sign unto you," he said with a smile that could melt the hardest of hearts. "You will recognize Him thus: in a poor stable behind Bethlehem you will find a Baby in swaddling clothes, in a manger for animals, as there was no room for the Messiah in the City of David."

I was trying to comprehend all that I was hearing. No room for the Messiah? What an outrage! At that moment I wanted nothing more than to find Him and honor Him in any way that I could. But before I could think any further, the angel was joined by what must have been the entire host of heaven. All of them bright, powerful and beautiful heavenly beings, and as they descended upon the earth like a great whirlwind. The air was filled with the other-worldly splendor of their ethereal singing. They were singing the songs of heaven as they illuminated the night skies above with the glory and light of their presence. These were songs of praise sung by lips of purity that had known not sin. Truly, I thought, how pleasing such a magnificent chorus must sound to the ears of Almighty God.

And then, very subtly at first, and soon more swiftly, the great light before us began to diffuse. With it, the sound of their singing receded from our hearing until it faded away completely and we were once again left alone.

Anam realized that the others were listening as intently as he was to Eli's story, hanging onto his every word. It was clear that they all considered this a momentous and most blessed event. Some of them were weeping uncontrollably. These were big, brawny, rough herdsmen—weeping! And yet the people of Bethlehem claim that they are lying about the angelic visit. If it were a lie, why would they get so emotional when remembering the event? For the first time Anam began to wonder if their story was true. And if so, what did it all mean? He leaned in closer as Eli continued his story...

After the angels ascended back to heaven, I slowly made my way back onto my feet, as did the others. Within minutes we were all murmuring to one another, trying to decide what we should do, still shocked by what we had all just beheld. "We must go and find this stable at once!" I declared. The others agreed, intent to obey God's word. We left the animals behind. We knew that the task before us was far more important.

Simon then told us about an encounter he had had earlier in the day. He had seen a woman, heavy with child, soon to give birth. She and her husband were looking for lodging in town, but were unable to find any. So Simon told them about the stable. We all agreed that this must be the child the angel had told us about. We gathered up whatever provisions we could offer to this little family and set off in great haste toward the stable, which was only a short distance. One of us brought a sheep with swollen udders for milk.

We quickly made our way over the hills with the light of a great star, much brighter than any I had ever seen, to guide our way. Bypassing the sleeping town, we approached the stable from the rear so that we would not be spotted. When we arrived at the stable, none of us seemed to have the courage to go inside and announce our arrival. The others began to prod me saying, "Eli, you were the first to see the angel. You go in first."

I took a step forward, then stopped dead in my tracks. "But, but I do not know what to say," I stammered.

"Just tell them that the angel sent us here, and we have come to help them, and to pay homage to the newborn King," said Benjamin, the eldest of our group.

Still I hesitated. I knew what we were doing was righteous, but all of my life I had never been in the presence of greatness, and I was too afraid.

"Then at least go and take a look inside. Be very quiet," Benjamin whispered, *"and they will not even know that you are here."*

The others all nodded their heads in silent agreement. Feeling obligated, I gathered up my courage and crept toward a tiny opening from where I could see the inside of the stable. I felt Benjamin's hot breath upon my ear in stark contrast to the chilly night air. "Well," he asked impatiently, "what do you see, lad?"

"I see a young woman. Ah, she is as beautiful as the angels. Her baby is nearby, crying. She is speaking to him in a way that almost sounds like singing." I didn't know exactly how to describe it to the others, but it was a voice unlike any I had ever heard before, and it was clear to me that there was a bond between mother and child that was even stronger than that which is ordained by nature. Her words were comforting to the tiny babe, and as she picked him up and held him in her arms, he cooed in contentment.

Benjamin nudged me, whispering in my ear, "Go inside and introduce yourself to them, and then we too will come in and join with you."

50

But before I had a chance to move, a tall man appeared in front of the entrance. He wore the humble garment of an ordinary man, yet something about him was of a regal bearing. The man eyed me with suspicion, and then he looked past my shoulder at the others standing behind me lighting the night with their torches. "Who is there? Tell me your names," he demanded, blocking the entrance protectively.

My voice caught in my throat a moment before I finally managed to say, "Sir, we are shepherds. We have come bringing food and some wool for you." Then I added, as reverently as I could, "And most importantly, to worship the Savior."

A smile of recognition crossed the man's handsome face. "I am Joseph," he said, and he stepped aside to let us in.

The others followed timidly, and we made our way to the young mother and child. The infant was falling asleep in her arms as she sat perched on the edge of a bale of hay. "I am Mary," she said softly. "We are pleased to have visitors."

One of the younger boys walked up to her and deposited some of the food at her feet. She smiled warmly at the youth and said, "God will remember your kindness, young man." Then she looked at the rest of us with that same sweet smile. "As He will for all of you."

I then remembered the wool that we had brought with us. I removed it from the sack we carried it in and laid it at her feet. "Mother, please take this lambskin blanket. It will keep your precious son warm. I prepared it for my own child who is about to be born, but I want you to have it… for the Savior," I said.

She reached out and patted my hand warmly. Her skin was smooth and soft. "Yet another gesture of kindness. We have no way to repay you," she said as she wrapped the baby in the blanket.

Joseph was standing nearby. "That is true," he said. "All we can offer is our sincere gratitude."

Then Benjamin said, "There is, in fact, one thing that you can do for us."

Joseph looked at him curiously.

"Allow us to worship the Savior," said Benjamin, his old eyes filling with tears. "I, like so many who have gone before me, have awaited this day for so long. And now it has come at last."

Gently rocking the tiny baby in her arms, Mary looked at the group of us assembled before them and asked, "How is it that you men have knowledge of this?"

Benjamin began to speak, but by this point he had become too overrun with emotion. I spoke up, and told her the entire story of the angels and the message they had delivered unto us.

Upon hearing my words, she smiled knowingly at Joseph, and he returned the gesture. "Yes, you men will be the first of many to hear the truth," he said. "What the prophets of old foretold has come to pass this very night."

All of us went down on our knees and vowed our obedience and loyalty to the newborn King. We venerated him, and sang holy songs in his honor. It was a wondrous time for all of us. We asked Mary to remember our names when her son the Messiah comes of age. It was a privilege beyond measure to be the first to come and adore him.

Mary looked upon all of us, one at a time, with eyes full of love and compassion. "Tell me your names, each of you."

One by one, we humbly stepped forward and she allowed us to kiss the hem of the garment of her child, Jesus. We each told her our name as we did so. Before we finally left, she said to us, "The Lord will be with you all of your lives. Come hardship, oppression, or any difficulty, rest assured that He will always be right by your side."

We turned to her husband Joseph. He nodded his agreement, smiled at us and said, "Go in peace."

And with that we set off once again into the starry darkness and back toward our sheep. I shall never forget that special night in that little stable. Our encounter with Jesus the Messiah, Mary his Mother, and her beloved spouse Joseph blessed all of us. Even all of these many years later, nothing else in life can compare with it. It changed us forever.

Chapter Six

For Anam, this had been the most amazing evening of his life. What he found most remarkable were the words attributed to the angel by Eli. They were, in effect, the very same words written upon the lambskin that was the only clue to his birth. "Glory to God in the Highest Heaven and peace on earth to men of good will, through Jesus Christ Who was born of Mary in a stable in Bethlehem and Who, wrapped in swaddling clothes, was in a manger, He Who is the Savior of the world."

This same Jesus seemed to be at the heart of so much controversy! The shepherds adored him and claimed that he was the promised Messiah. Yet the people of Bethlehem reviled him and refused to even speak his name. Anam was confused. What was the truth? How did this all fit into his own life? Why was this mysterious Jesus so important?

Anam was, however, now very sure of one thing. These shepherds were not at all who he originally thought they were. He could hear the sincerity in their voices as each man stood up and gave his testimony about that night three decades earlier. These were not the drunken recollections of a vagabond group of reprobates. Nay, to the contrary, the shepherds had demonstrated to Anam that they were quite genuine about what they believed. Of course, he supposed that it was possible that somehow they were mistaken. Maybe there was some sort of logical explanation for what they had seen. Yet, whatever it was that had really transpired that night some thirty years ago, at the very least Anam no longer harbored any doubt that these men were honest and gentle souls who truly believed every word that they had uttered.

They had finished their gathering with fervent prayers and songs of praise to God before retiring to their tents for the evening. Eli was even kind enough to offer Anam a place to sleep in his own tent, which the young man gratefully accepted. He had so many questions he wanted to ask Eli, but he had no eloquence of speech and felt unsure of himself, not knowing exactly how he should phrase things. It reminded him of Moses, who said he was not a good speaker, but God provided him his brother Aaron to compensate for that deficiency. *But I have no "real" brothers to speak for me…and surely, I am no Moses to begin with!*

As Anam wrestled with what to say, he soon heard the soft snoring of his tent-mate. He looked over and saw the old man fast asleep, his mouth slightly ajar. The slow and steady sound reminded him of his father Micah. It had only been a few days since leaving home, yet he missed him so already. Though not his father by blood, this man who found him as a baby and a stranger had shown him genuine paternal love for his entire life. Was this a betrayal, seeking to find his "true" father? On the one hand, it felt that way, and it hurt to think that he might be offending Micah. Yet, he had given Anam his blessing to go on this journey, so he knew that the guilt he was feeling was unjustified.

Why, then, he asked himself, did he feel such tension at this very moment? Perhaps the idea of at last finding out the truth about his origins frightened him. After all, his entire life he had gone about carrying this great mystery within himself. In a way, it had become a part of him. Now that was all about to change. Would it mean he was no longer part of Micah's family? Would this new revelation change his life in ways that he did not want? His heart was filled with the joy of anticipation along with the dread of the unknown.

He decided it would be best to sleep, yet sleep escaped him. Finally, he got up and quietly slipped outside of the tent. The night was ablaze with starlight, and cold. Anam walked to the far edge of the encampment, past the sleeping sheep, and he found a small cluster of trees. He wondered if perhaps this was the very spot where the shepherds had first seen the angel. No longer did he think in terms of they "claimed" they saw an angel, because he honestly believed that their words were true. There was nothing deceitful that he could discern about these men.

Anam cast his eyes upon the great constellations of blinking stars shining down from the vault of heaven above.

There was no angel out here in these fields tonight. None that he could see, at least. His father Micah had often told him that multitudes of God's angels roamed the earth at all times, offering their protection and guidance to all of the righteous. He would frequently imagine that there were guardian angels following his every movement, keeping him safe from enemies and helping him to avoid pitfalls. The thought had always brought him great comfort and peace of mind.

But the angel described by Eli and the other shepherds was of a visible form, or at least he revealed himself in such a way. He was in the form of a man, though glorified far beyond that of mere flesh and blood. If only such a being would come to him now, surely one so powerful could answer all of his questions. He looked up into the heavens almost as if expecting a vision. Alas, the skies remained in a natural state. No singing choirs of the heavenly host, no celestial lights. Just a cold winter's night, and one man standing alone with his unanswered questions.

To keep warm, he ambled about the gently rolling meadows and rubbed his hands together. His tired mind wandered, meandering its way back toward the one period in his life when he thought that, just maybe, he could find true happiness and contentment. In assisting his father with his merchant business, they had on numerous occasions traveled to a great trading center many miles away on the shores of the sea. It was here that his father was engaged in commerce with a very wealthy man named Isaac, with whom he traded all kinds of valuable goods from ports both near and far. Both men prospered much from these lucrative transactions.

On one of these trips, Anam had occasion to meet with a young woman whom he later found out was Isaac's daughter. She had a keen sense of math, and though it was not at all the norm for women to do such work, this remarkable girl helped her father to keep accurate accounts for his business. Anam learned that her name was Judith, and he was smitten on first laying eyes upon her. Such a smooth complexion had she, and thick, dark hair, finer than he had ever seen before. Beyond her beauty, there was a wit and intelligence about her that he found intriguing. The two struck up a friendship and before long, the inevitable flame of young love was ignited.

Wanting to do what was proper and fitting, and what his heart was calling him to do, Anam had gone to his father Micah and told him that he would like to have permission to ask for this girl's hand in marriage.

Anam recalled the old man's reaction as if it were only yesterday. His expression somber, Micah slowly shook his head and said, "I am afraid that will not be possible, my son."

Anam's countenance shrank into sadness. "But why?" he cried. "Is she yet betrothed to another?"

"No. I am friends with her father and I know that not to be so."

Befuddled and desperately disappointed, Anam asked, "Is it something I have done? Did I offend her or her family in any way?"

"No."

Both were silent, until Micah finally did what he had to do and told him the truth. "Anam, there are certain things in life that do not seem fair. It is best that you come to know this at a young age. The girl's father would never permit you to marry his daughter. His bloodline is of a long and noble heritage. He will see to it that her husband is a man whose seed can continue that noble bloodline."

In his innocence, Anam had naively said, "But, father, our family is likewise of noble heritage. Can I not, therefore, be such a man?"

Micah put his hand on Anam's shoulder. "You know that ever since I first took you home, I have considered you my son. And so I shall, till my dying breath." He sighed heavily before continuing. "But, I must tell you, the world does not see it the same way. Your real father is unknown to all, so we cannot say who you truly are. Your children would have no heritage. Perhaps if there is a girl whose family is of no distinction, then we…"

Anam had politely and obediently listened to the rest of what his father had to say, but so far as he was concerned the damage had already been done. Even now, many years later, Micah's words painfully echoed through the corridors of his mind: "Your real father is unknown." As Anam shivered in the cold night air, he hugged himself for warmth and began to make his way back to the camp. He wondered if he would ever be able to shake off the feeling that he was not whole, that he was like a tree without any roots. Such a tree, he knew, if it could exist at all, would not survive very long. It would have no way to sustain itself. It would wither away and die, and nobody would even remember that it was ever there to begin with. At times like this, he felt as if his very soul were without roots, drifting aimlessly, awaiting a future of nothingness.

As he shuffled along he at last came to the tent of Eli. To his surprise, there was the faint flickering of light inside. He poked his head through the folds of the tent and found the old man hunched over large scrolls of parchment, a single lamp his only source of light. His thoughts immediately turned to his father Micah, who also had a great devotion to the Word of God.

"I beg your pardon," Anam said quietly, bowing his head as he stepped inside. "I did not mean to intrude."

Eli looked up at him. "No intrusion at all, my son," he said. "As you age, you will find that it is difficult to maintain sleep throughout the night." The old shepherd smiled and added, "Though it seems you yourself are not able to sleep either."

Anam took a step closer and Eli beckoned him to sit down, which he did. "I could not sleep, not after all I have heard this evening."

His face beaming, Eli said, "So, you enjoyed hearing of our miraculous encounter?"

Though he would not have quite phrased it that way himself, to a certain degree it was true. Anam was indeed intrigued by this story of the angel and the newborn King. But the evil that followed afterwards remained for him a stumbling block and source of great pain.

"Yes, I did," he said. "One part in particular. Where you recited the words that the angel from on high had spoken to you."

Eli was quiet as he waited for him to continue. Anam slowly reached into his bag and carefully, with reverence, he retrieved the lambskin blanket and unfolded it. Then he held it before Eli's eyes. Without being asked, the old man read the words aloud. The hint of a smile crossed his face, but he was quite serious as he asked, "Where did you find this?"

"I did not find it. My father… well, Micah, the man I call my father, found it wrapped around me when I was but an infant. The woman we presume was my mother lay dead beside me. It appeared she gave her life trying to save mine. And these words…how do they connect me or my family to this Jesus? I feel as if I have been drawn to you to find the answer."

Looking up toward the top of the tent, Eli closed his eyes and muttered a prayer of thanks. "Indeed, Anam, you have been sent here for the answers you seek. It is all becoming very clear to me now. I knew your father. In fact, I knew him very well."

Anam's eyes widened. In all of his life, this was the first person he had ever met with direct knowledge about one of his parents. He could feel his heart beat faster with anticipation. Eli did not make him wait a moment longer.

"Your father was my master. I used to care for his sheep before the calamity."

"Please, tell me more," Anam said with excitement.

"How fortunate I am to be able to tell you, his son, what a wonderful man he was," said Eli, doing his best to fight back tears. "Anam, he loved both you and your mother very much. The two of you were the light of his life, and I so vividly recall how he beamed with pride and joy over your birth, his first born and only son. Ahhh, he was such a happy man. Following the custom of our people, he performed the rite of circumcision on you and gave you a name. He named you Stephen."

Anam was fixated by every word. One of the long lost secrets of his life had at last been revealed. He finally knew what his real name was. But there was still so much more to learn. He listened with rapt attention as Eli continued.

"Your father's name was Issachar, and he was a priest. He was a very important man in the town of Bethlehem. Yea, he was the leader of the synagogue, the man who led worship services. He would officiate at marriages, funerals and all of the religious festivals and holy days. Issachar was the man who people would come to when they needed advice, and all respected him for his wisdom and his knowledge of the things of God."

His mind whirling with a thousand questions, Anam asked first the one question that he had wondered about the most often over the years. "The woman we believe was my mother seems to have died protecting me. But what happened to my father? Did he survive?"

Up until now, Eli had seemed quite pleased to recount the details of his father's life to Anam. But his smile turned downward as he cleared his throat and spoke. "The sad answer is no, he did not. The relatives of those killed in the massacre took his life in revenge."

With those words, the last vestige of hope Anam had that his father might yet be alive vanished into thin air. He soon felt his sadness turning to anger. "But you said he was a leader in the town, well-respected for his wisdom. Why, then, would they kill him? I do not understand."

Eli sighed and nodded toward the scrolls laid out before him. "What happened to your father is the same as happened to these holy men of old," he said, gesturing to the parchment. "He met his death for proclaiming the words of God."

Confused, Anam said, "My father was a prophet?"

Eli considered it for a moment. "Not in the strictest sense of the word, perhaps. But the principle, I believe, is the same. Just as many of God's holy prophets were killed by the very people to whom they were sent to speak the truth, so your father died for proclaiming to the people of Bethlehem what he knew to be true."

Now it was all becoming clear. "This has to do with Jesus, doesn't it?"

With a nod, Eli confirmed it was true. "Yes," he said. "Let me explain. You see, I was close to your father for many years. I knew him well. He was a just man, and was kind to me. In fact, he was one of the few people I have met who did not seem to care about one's station in life. He treated all with the same respect and dignity. So after our miraculous encounter with the angel, and upon visiting the newborn King and his family, the first man I went to see to announce these wondrous events was your father."

Anam said, "And since he considered you a friend, he believed you?"

With a wide smile, the old shepherd said, "Oh no. That was not the kind of man your father was. He had no reason to disbelieve me, but when it came to the things of God, he went to God Himself for confirmation."

A look of confusion swept over Anam's face in the tent's dim lamp-light. "What do you mean he went to God Himself?"

"Let me explain. First, he came with me to see the child for himself. Soon he became friendly with Joseph and Mary, and came to realize that they were special people in God's plan. But even then he was still not fully satisfied. You see, Anam, your father was very learned in the Torah. It was said that he could recite every word of it by memory, and I believe it. He scoured through the ancient prophecies for confirmation of the angel's words."

"Did he find them to be true?"

"Indeed he did," said Eli with a smile. "Yes, I remember as if it were yesterday, the day he stood up in front of the congregation assembled before him at the synagogue and proclaimed that the day of redemption promised by our God had come at last. He told the assembly that the holy words inspired by God himself in the sacred writings had confirmed it to be true."

"And did they believe my father?" Anam could feel his breathing quicken its pace. It felt strange to be calling this man he had never met by the name of "father." Strange but wonderful.

Eli said, "At first they did. They rejoiced in the good news he brought to them, and considered it to be a great honor that Bethlehem was the Savior's place of birth. But then…" he stopped as his voice began to crack.

"Please, Eli. I must hear the rest of the story," Anam pleaded.

"And then came the great and terrible tragedy. Word of these events reached King Herod, and in his jealousy, and zeal to protect his own power, he unleashed the wrath of his soldiers on the defenseless hamlet of Bethlehem."

"I…I was told when I was in town how terrible this bloody violence was," Anam said. "All of those precious little babies so senselessly murdered…"

The old man's eyes were full of pain as the memory of it surged through his heart and mind. "It came to be known as the Slaughter of the Innocents. And afterwards, in their anger and grief, the townspeople went to your father Issachar the priest, and asked him if he still believed in this Jesus. They angrily jeered him and demanded that he renounce the name of this outsider who had brought nothing but death and destruction to their once peaceful community."

Anam was silent. He was going to ask if his father then denied Jesus, but he felt that he already knew the answer.

"Your father was a very brave man, Anam," said Eli. "Spurred on by rabble rousers, a bloodthirsty gang of grieving relatives of the dead gathered outside of his synagogue and demanded that he curse the name of Jesus, and repent of calling him the Messiah. But your father steadfastly refused, telling them that even death could not shake his convictions. The brutal mob picked up stones and without mercy they assailed him unto death. Then, in their murderous fury the rabid crowd burned the synagogue to the ground with him inside. The ruins of this once splendid and holy building lay decaying on the ground to this very day."

The sad story tore at Anam's heart. But there was still more that he needed to know. "Eli, my mother died also. Was it as I have always thought…did she lose her life trying to save mine?"

"Yes, that is exactly how it happened. Your father had been out of town just before the massacre took place. He was in Jerusalem tending to the synagogue's business in the Temple. I knew your mother very well too. She was a sweet and kindly woman, with a heart as big as I have ever seen, and her love for you was beyond measure. More than anything else, she wanted you to have a chance at life. I came and warned her what was happening, and that the soldiers were coming, and she fled in the darkness of the night with only the clothes on her back. The only possession she had with her...was that blanket that you have shown me this night."

Anam's eyes became like large saucers. "You knew about this blanket? Please, tell me of its origin."

"It was the very lambskin we shepherds had given to Jesus on the night of his birth. Mary the mother of Jesus wrapped that him in it for many cold nights. Yet, by the time you were born, Jesus had outgrown it. Mary was a most loving and hospitable woman, and she had become friends with your mother, so she gave your mother the blanket as a gift shortly after you were born. Your father wrote those words on the lambskin in my presence. He wanted to write down the words just as the angel had said them, so I repeated those words to him as he wrote."

To think that he and Jesus had shared the same blanket as newborn babes, and his father was a believer that this child was indeed the Messiah. Anam just knew that there had to be some sort of connection between himself and Jesus. He couldn't explain it, but he could feel it in the deepest part of his soul.

Eli said, "Your father loved you very much, Anam, and in fact he said that if anything ever happened to him, I should be the one to tell you about Jesus when you were old enough to understand. But then you disappeared, and we all assumed that you were dead along with so many others."

Anam felt a shiver tremble throughout his body. All of this news was just too incredible for him to absorb all at once.

The aging shepherd reached out and placed his hand on Anam's shoulder. "Yet now, in his own perfect timing, the Lord has brought you here to me."

Chapter Seven

The next morning Anam decided it was time for him to leave. He had discovered what he came here to learn. He now not only knew his "real" name, but he also knew the identity of his father and mother, and how and why they died. Yet obtaining this knowledge in no way put his restless heart at ease. In fact, it led to an inner turmoil unlike anything he had ever experienced before. It raised questions about this newly revealed father and his beliefs, and forced him to struggle within himself regarding his own beliefs and how he should live the rest of his life.

Anam thanked Eli and the other shepherds for their hospitality as he prepared for the long journey home. Samuel brought him a large sack containing food and other provisions to make his trip more comfortable. "You are too kind," Anam said. "I cannot repay you."

"Your smile and the knowledge that you will have a full stomach as you travel is thanks enough for me, friend," Samuel replied.

Eli embraced Anam and said, "Truly, your coming here was directed by God. Of that, I am quite certain."

"As am I," said Anam softly, almost in a whisper.

"Here," Eli said, "I want you to take this with you." He handed Anam a large scroll, which had been thoughtfully rolled up and was held tight by a silver clasp.

Taking it into his hands, Anam asked, "What is this?"

"This was a gift from your father. He gave it to me as his way of thanking me for coming to him first with the blessed news from the lips of the angel. It is something so special to me that I have hidden it away in my heart. Now it is time to pass it on to you, young man."

"No, Eli, I cannot accept this. You said it was special to you. You mustn't…"

"Yes, but I no longer have need of the physical part of the gift. What is of the spirit is spiritual and will stay with me forever."

Anam did not fully understand Eli's words, but he would not dispute them further. He simply said, "Thank you," and with one final round of farewells, he was off.

It was a warm and sunny afternoon as Anam once again found himself back on the main road. Though he had no intention of stopping this time, to get home he would have to again pass through the town of Bethlehem. As he did, it suddenly came to him what Eli had said about the synagogue where his father was killed: the ruins remained to this day. He came upon a farmer repairing a fence upon his property. He approached the middle aged man and said, "Good sir, if you will, please direct me toward the ruins of the synagogue that once stood in this town thirty years ago."

The farmer looked at him suspiciously. "It was destroyed when I was but a young child. Why do you want to know where it is, stranger? It's just an old pile of rubble and ashes now."

Anam looked at him with longing in his eyes. "It is a difficult story to explain, but, please, if possible I would be most grateful for your assistance."

After considering it for a moment, the farmer shrugged and said, "Well, I suppose no harm can come from it," and he directed Anam to a spot near the edge of some woods at the outer fringes of town. Anam thanked the man and was on his way.

As he made his way toward the ruined sanctuary, Eli's words played over and over again in the chambers of his mind. Anam's father Issachar had obviously been a very brave man. He died standing up for what he believed. But this faith that Issachar had in Jesus, what sense did it make? After all, this Jesus was a tiny newborn baby. How could his father be so certain that he would grow up to the Messiah? A child could take all different kinds of paths in life. Anam couldn't imagine how his father could have such steadfast certitude that this boy would go on to greatness.

In fact, what reason was there to believe that he had survived at all? According to everybody he had spoken to, the soldiers came and killed all of the male babies soon after the birth of Jesus. Since it was Jesus whose life they sought, wouldn't it have only made sense that they did indeed find and kill him? If that were so, then his father had died for nothing. He had been killed defending one who was already dead!

Anam turned off the main road where the helpful farmer had told him there was an old, smaller side road that led to the ruins of the synagogue. Birds went about their daily business, fluttering from one treetop to the next in the sunshine, oblivious to the feelings that were tearing this human being's heart asunder. He envied them sometimes. The lives of animals seemed so simple and carefree compared to the complex and often troubling ways of men.

His mind again turned to Jesus. Even if he did somehow survive the massacre, what reason was there for Anam to believe that he was truly the Messiah? Yes, this good man he now knew to be his father firmly believed Jesus was the Promised One of Israel, as did the shepherds. But that was so many years ago, and nothing had been heard from this Jesus since, at least as far as Anam was aware. Was it possible that they were wrong? Could the townspeople of Bethlehem been right after all? If so, then the gullibility of his father and the shepherds believing what was false had led to all of that death and destruction. Maybe the shepherds' persistent faith only proved that they were stubborn old men who, out of guilt or pride or both, refused to admit they had been wrong. Then again, their belief seemed so pure. Searching deep within his soul, Anam felt that every time he was coming to a conclusion, doubts and new questions would begin his quest for answers all over again.

The path became overgrown with weeds and seemed to be heading nowhere. Anam was getting hot and tired and he began to think maybe he should just forget this foolish idea and head directly for home. But then as he rounded a bend, he saw it. Laid out before him was a clearing, and as he drew closer he could see that the foundation of a large building was still there, though now it was just an enormous hole in the ground. Inside the hole were burnt slabs of wood, charred black and rotting from years of decay and exposure to the elements. "So this was your holy place, my father," Anam whispered as a light wind tousled his hair.

He walked closer to inspect the place in more detail. There was not much left to it. The charred remains of some furniture, such as benches where the congregation must have once sat for worship services, were scattered about, but there was not much more. Clearly, this was a place that mankind had turned its back on a long time ago. It seemed like the kind of lonely, deserted place that time itself had forgotten. Anam looked about and noticed that there weren't even any birds here, even though they were plentiful less than a mile down the road. Both man and beast had forsaken this place, he thought.

Near what he surmised was the entrance he found a large boulder. He sat down upon it and closed his eyes. "Issachar my Father," he said into the whispering wind, "I know in my heart you were a good man. And I believe Eli that you and mother wanted only the best for me. But now I need your guidance. Is there any sign that you can give me to lead me to the truth?"

Only the soft breeze replied.

Anam stood up and stretched and decided to leave. As much as he wanted to stay and somehow find out more about his past, this place was not providing any answers. Just as he was about to leave, the sack that he had placed on the boulder fell off and tumbled to the ground. He turned to pick it up, and he noticed that the large scroll Eli had given him had slipped out of the sack and the silver clasp that held it shut had come unhinged. He stooped down to pick it up, and his eye landed upon something in the writing that captured his attention. He sat back down upon the boulder, gathered the scroll up in his hands and began to read.

In large, carefully drawn, almost delicate script were the words, "The Testimony of Issachar." This was the gift that his father had given to Eli, and now this long since dead man's son was about to read it. The parchment scrolls were actually references from the ancient books of the prophets. Anam's eyes widened as he read the story that they told. Issachar was proclaiming that Jesus was the Messiah, and he was using the words of the prophets to demonstrate that Jesus was indeed the one of whom they had written. The evidence his father has amassed was remarkable. For example, in the Book of Isaiah he read, **Therefore the Lord himself shall give you a sign; Behold, a virgin shall conceive, and bear a son, and shall call his name Immanuel.** In all of the accounts he had heard from the shepherds, there had never been any doubt but that Mary the mother of Jesus had been a virgin.

Remarkably, even the shepherds themselves were foretold in the ancient Scriptures. In the Book of Psalms, Issachar had noted the following: **They that dwell in the wilderness shall bow before him; and his enemies shall lick the dust.**

Anam was especially startled to read the prophecy of Micah, for whom his surrogate father had been named. The following verse was inscribed upon the parchment: **But thou, Bethlehem Ephratah, though thou be little among the thousands of Judah, yet out of thee shall he come forth unto me that is to be ruler in Israel; whose goings forth have been from of old, from everlasting.**

This oracle had been written many centuries earlier, and yet the accuracy of this prophecy was uncanny. Anam concluded that these signs, along with many others that Issachar had compiled and recorded, could point to no other than Jesus—the Messiah. He kept reading for many hours, for so long in fact that he lost track of the time.

At long last Anam came to the end of his reading and he carefully rolled up the scroll and held it shut with the silver clasp. He kissed the coarse parchment before reverently placing it back inside the sack of provisions Samuel had given to him. The weight of the evidence his father Issachar the priest had amassed attesting that Jesus was the Messiah left Anam with a profound respect for this man he had never known. "Yet your blood flows through my veins," he whispered. His father was a wise man indeed. He searched the word of God and when the Messiah came, he was ready to welcome him. His faith in God and in the prophets was unshakable, and he paid for it with his life. But what of me? Anam asked himself. *Now that I also know of this great truth, what shall I do with it? Do I remain silent, or was I too chosen to be a witness?* Unlike his father, Anam had never been in the actual presence of this Jesus, however, so perhaps his own life had no great purpose. Now that he had learned the truth about his parents, maybe he should just go home, settle down with some nice peasant girl, and live out the remainder of his days.

Ready now to move on again, Anam decided that he would not leave town before stopping in to thank Johanan, the innkeeper, who was kind enough to tell him where he could meet the shepherds at their winter pasture. Micah had always taught him the importance of showing gratitude to those who help us, so the gesture only seemed fitting. By the time he made his way to the now familiar inn, it was late afternoon and the sun was slowly descending upon the western horizon. He entered the inn and found Johanan looking much happier than when he had last visited. This time he was at the dinner table with a woman. Matronly and strong looking, clearly she was his wife. Both of them turned when they heard Anam rap lightly on the door.

"We have a visitor," said the woman.

Johanan broke into a wide smile. "Ah, I know this gentleman. In fact, my love, this is the man I was telling you about earlier."

Anam was more than a little surprised. *Why would they be talking about me?* he wondered. He entered the room and sat down at the table when Johanan insisted he have dinner with them. The innkeeper had introduced the woman as his wife Raisa. "When I was here a few days ago, ma'am, you were sick and unable to join your husband for the evening meal," said Anam. "I am glad to see that you are better now."

"Praise be to God," said Raisa. "I had been told there was no chance of recovery. They said that this was a sickness unto death; yea, they had even prepared my burial plot. But in his goodness, the Lord sent to us a healer, and now I feel as if I am a healthy young girl again."

This was remarkable. Anam had known that prayers for the sick were always a part of sacred tradition, but he had never heard of such a miraculous healing. "That is indeed wonderful news," he said. "Please tell me how it came about."

Johanan looked Anam directly in the eye and said, "You may find this hard to believe, but earlier today a group of strangers came into Bethlehem. Their leader was a rabbi whose reputation as a miracle worker has been growing now for some time. Normally, I put no stock in such claims. Yet with my beloved Raisa so near to death, I felt I had no choice but to seek him out. I invited him into my house, and with the laying on of his hands, in an instant Raisa arose from her bed and was cured. This rabbi said to her, 'Your faith has healed you, woman.' It was absolutely stunning."

Anam wasn't sure what to say, but Johanan's next words were even more amazing. His voice became solemn as he spoke.

"The man, Anam, was the one they call Jesus."

A lump formed in Anam's throat. This was almost too much to bear. "Jesus, the very one whose name you refused to hear?" he said.

Johanan confirmed it by nodding his head. "Yes, it was he. Jesus and some of his followers were passing through town, and he was showing them the place of his birth. I now realize that all that I had believed about him was not true. The massacre was not his fault. It happened due to the acts of evil men who were jealous of his power and wanted to kill him. But he survived their wicked plot, and has lived on into manhood to do good deeds and preach salvation. This man, I now believe, truly has been sent by God to deliver his people."

Raisa said to Anam, "My husband was telling me that you had a lambskin inscribed with the words of an angel announcing the birth of Jesus. He seems to be connected to your own birth in some mysterious sort of way."

"Yes. Yes, I now believe that he is," said Anam, thrilled to think that Jesus was now at this very moment so nearby. He felt as if his life would never be fulfilled if he did not find him. He turned to Johanan and said, "I would like to meet this Jesus too. Where might I find him?"

The old man explained that Jesus and his followers did not stay in Bethlehem very long. Jesus had wanted to show them the stable where he was born, and then the group was going to find the shepherds at their winter pasture. They were in and out of town too quickly to encounter any trouble with the locals. This was clearly a man of peace who sought to avoid violence and strife. It had been only a few hours since they departed, and if Anam hurried he might be able to catch up with them. Johanan even told him of a shortcut through some rough country that would save him a significant amount of time.

Anam thanked Johanan and his wife for their hospitality. Then he set off down the road again, hoping to find out at last if all that he had now come to believe was really true.

Chapter Eight

Anam ran as fast as he could down a small, barely discernable path outside of town, and arrived at the shepherds' encampment just as dusk enveloped the countryside. His arms and legs bore multiple cuts and scrapes from the thorns and branches that covered many sections of the rough trail. Yet he paid them no attention as he came upon Jonas, the young shepherd he'd first encountered upon his arrival the day before, cleaning up the remnants of the evening meal. "Jonas, my friend," he called out. "I am so glad to see you."

Jonas spun around, surprised. "Anam! We thought you had returned to your own town. Is there something wrong?"

"No, nothing is wrong. I just need to know. Is he here yet?"

Jonas cocked his head. "Is who here?"

Anam then knew that Jesus and his friends must not have arrived yet. With the shortcut he took, he would be in time. "You'll see," he said smiling. "Where is Eli?"

"Down at the stream with the others gathered to wash up, and then to say the evening prayer. I am going to join them as soon as I finish up here."

Anam began helping him put away the cookware and utensils. "Jonas, my friend," he said. "I believe tonight all of our prayers will be answered."

Within ten minutes they had completed their task and walked to the little stream to meet Eli and the other shepherds. All of them were astonished to see Anam return to them so quickly. Especially Eli. "Is something wrong, my son? Why have you not gone home?"

Before he could reply, Samuel pointed and said, "Look. Some men are coming down from that hilltop in the distance." Indeed, three strangers walked toward them. The setting sun behind them cast an unnatural glow around their silhouettes.

"Let's continue with our prayers, but keep a watchful eye as they approach," Eli warned. And then he turned to Anam and said, "Why don't you join us? We say this prayer every morning and evening…to remember what the angel said. I think you will recognize it."

The shepherds stood in a circle as they reverently recited words that had long been etched into their memories. "Glory to God in the Highest Heaven and peace on earth to men of good will, through Jesus Christ Who was born of Mary in a stable in Bethlehem and Who, wrapped in swaddling clothes, was in a manger, He Who is the Savior of the world." Just as they finished, the three strangers appeared over a small rise just a few yards away.

All eyes turned to face the newcomers, none of whom

looked familiar. The small band descended the hill and their leader, a sturdy looking man with longish brown hair, a thick beard and piercing brown eyes said, "Peace be with you, my friends."

The shepherds were surprised by such a greeting, so long had it been since a stranger had called them "friends." There was an awkward silence and then Eli asked, "Who are you?"

Without hesitation the stranger smiled broadly and said, "One who loves you." And then the stranger asked, "What was that prayer we heard as we were approaching?"

Eli stared at the man for a moment. Though he had not laid eyes upon this man before, somehow there was something familiar about him. "It is a prayer taught to us by an angel of the Lord long ago. On a cold night, the angel appeared and the sky was as bright as day. The angel announced the birth of the Messiah in Bethlehem."

"Messiah? Is it this Jesus you mentioned in your prayer? Is he your Messiah?" The stranger was still smiling as he asked.

"Yes, my lord. His name is Jesus. We adored him as a newborn infant that night. Oh! He was so beautiful! And his mother ...!"

"And what happened to the baby? Does he yet live?"

"I wish we knew. He fled Bethlehem before Herod's slaughter, and we have no word of him since. We have been persecuted and treated like murderers, but it would all be worth it if we only knew he is alive. But even if we never see him again, we will continue saying to everyone who will listen, 'The Messiah is born. The Savior is in the world. Angels told us so, and angels do not lie.'" Eli grew more and more animated as he spoke. "And so every morning at sunrise, and every evening when the first star appears, we repeat the prayer the angel taught us, and ask God to show us our Jesus."

When Eli had finished, the stranger had a tear in his eye and he opened his arms as if embracing the entire group. In a strong, loving voice, he said, "God has answered your prayer tonight. It is I, Jesus."

"You? Oh! Lord!" All of the men fell to their knees. The old man kissed Jesus' feet as the tears flowed freely down his face. The others knelt with their eyes wide and their jaws open. Could this really be true? Had Jesus returned to them after all of these years? "I prayed I would live to see you again," Eli kept repeating to himself. "Now, even if I die I shall be content that I did not hope in vain."

After a short period of reunion, Jesus led them in prayer and introduced them to his two disciples, brothers named James and John. The group returned to the camp and a great bonfire was lit as all assembled sat and listened to every word that Jesus had to say. "You men should know that never have I forgotten you. Though a mere babe when you came to offer me your adoration and gifts, my mother has many times recounted to me the entire story of your visit and she wishes you to know that, to this very day, she fondly recalls your kindness."

Eli said, "It is we who are in her debt, Master. We who were there all recall the splendor of her grace. We were privileged to have been witnesses to the miraculous circumstances of your birth. Please tell me, if I should be so bold to ask, why were we chosen for such an honor, and not the important men? We are but humble shepherds."

Jesus smiled upon him. He made eye contact with the two disciples he had brought with him, James and John. "There is a lesson here for all," he said. "In my kingdom, greatness is not measured as it is by the standards of this world. Those who have labored righteously in humility shall be richly rewarded by my Father. And many whom this world consider great shall not."

The disciple named John said to Eli, "We have heard the story of how a great massacre took place here. It seems the people of Bethlehem hold you in scorn and contempt, having blamed you for the tragedy."

Sitting quietly by Eli's side, Anam was taking in every word that was uttered very carefully. John's question went to the heart of the shepherd's dilemma, and Anam had now reached the point where he fully understood that they were blameless, yet continued to pay the price for an unjust accusation.

"It is true, my good man," Eli said to John. "But we are here to listen to the words of wisdom of Jesus, not the sad memories of an old man."

At that, Jesus looked directly into Eli's eyes, his own piercing brown eyes full of compassion. "Do not speak ill of yourself, Eli. Your story is important to me. In fact, that was one of my reasons for coming here. My mother has many times over the years told me how she has wondered what has become of you. Now you will speak it to me, and in turn, I to her."

Anam could tell that Eli was having a hard time continuing. He also noticed how patiently Jesus waited for the old man. Nothing in Jesus' demeanor seemed at all demanding, yet there was a sense about him that he was nonetheless in complete control. He was far different from anybody Anam had ever met before.

Finally, Eli collected himself and began to speak. "Your disciple is correct, Master, there was indeed a time of bloodshed and death. Your mother and her husband Joseph had already left with you, yet Herod and his minions were unaware. In their deadly quest, they searched high and low, and many met an untimely and cruel death at their wicked hands."

Jesus sat and listened as Eli wiped a tear from his eye. "The parents of these precious infants did all that they could to protect them. Many were slain by the sword in their futile efforts to halt the killing. I had a wife and child of my own. I was not home when the soldiers came. They…they…"

Sensing his pain, Jesus said, "There is no need to

continue. I know the rest of the story. You were not able to even bury them, as the people of the town cast stones at you and threatened your life."

The group was amazed. He seemed to know all about them even before they told him. Yet he had such tremendous compassion for them that he wanted to hear their own story in their own words, to let them know how much he cared. Anam could not take his eyes off of him.

Fighting back his tears, Eli said, "You know the truth indeed, Master. But I did not let it shake my faith in you. My fellow shepherds and I have gone all throughout the countryside and told all we have met what the angel told us. We feel compelled to announce to all of Israel that the Messiah has been born, and that a mighty angel of God has proclaimed it so. And we have done thus for all these many years."

James then spoke up for the first time. He said to Eli, "And how have they received your report? Do they believe?"

Sadly, Eli shook his head. "Most do not," he said. "In fact, because of the massacre, and our proclamation of Jesus as the Messiah, they have treated us as evildoers and outcasts ever since."

Jesus turned his head slowly until he had looked each of the shepherds directly in the eye. He did not, however, seem to be looking directly at Anam. To the shepherds he said, "You have suffered greatly all of these years for the sake of the truth. Though it may now seem that your efforts have been in vain, verily I say unto you they have not been in vain. For you have planted seeds amongst the people, preparing the way for the appearance of the Son of Man. Many will taste of salvation thanks to the bitter cup all of you have swallowed."

These words of Jesus were like the Balm of Gilead for the souls of these faithful men who had dedicated their lives to spreading the message they had received from God delivered by His angel. Almost as if on cue, the assembled group hailed Jesus with a mighty shout: "Praise be to God!" They had at last been vindicated. It was as if the years stolen by the locusts had been returned to them tenfold.

Jesus then spoke to the shepherds, individually and in small groups until late in the evening. It was as if he could peer into their very souls. He answered their questions and filled their hearts with God's love and the promise of his future Kingdom.

At long last all of the shepherds had returned to their tents in a festive mood, singing songs of praise and celebrating this momentous event. For the older shepherds, this was their second encounter with Jesus, having been with him thirty years prior as a newborn in that cold yet magical stable. For the younger shepherds, after hearing about him all of their lives, this was the first time they were actually in the Messiah's presence. But for all of them, it was an evening that would change their lives forever. He had touched them like the rays of the sun touching the earth on a warm spring morning.

Only Anam remained alone with Jesus. Anam had much to say, but he was so in awe of this man that the words would not come.

"You have come here for a reason, Anam," Jesus said. He had phrased it like a question, but to Anam's ears it sounded like a statement. And he knew that Jesus was right.

"Yes, rabbi," he said, "I came here to find out who I am. I did not know my name or my heritage, but now I do."

Jesus looked deep into Anam's eyes. "Yet your heart still is not at ease. You came seeking flesh and blood answers, and flesh and blood answers you have found."

He was right. Anam felt as if there was still a piece of the puzzle that was missing. "My entire life I wanted to know my name, and I thought when I came to know it I would come to know my purpose in life. But, alas, I find that I am still adrift and without direction."

Jesus said, "The Kingdom you have heard me speak about this night is not of this world. It is of the world to come. It is a great banquet to which all shall be called, though not all shall answer the call."

Anam knew the implications of his words without any further explanation. "Have I been called?" he asked.

"You have said it with your own lips," said Jesus.

"Am I to become your follower?" asked Anam.

"Is this what you believe, Stephen?"

This was the first time Anam had heard anybody call him by what he now knew was his rightful name. Without hesitation he replied, "My father before me searched the Scriptures and died for his belief in you, and the prophets of old foresaw your coming. Yes, I believe that you are the promised Messiah. But I do not know if I am worthy to follow you. I am a person of such little value."

Jesus smiled and compassionately reached out his hand to touch Anam's head. "Stephen, it is for such as you that I have come. You have come to know the life of the outcast, and your heart identifies with those who are in pain. You shall indeed follow me, and your deeds will earn you a special place in paradise, along with your father."

Anam marveled at these words. For the very first time, he felt as if he had a God-given purpose and mission for his life.

The next day, soon after rising, the two brothers, James and John, told the shepherds that their visit must now come to an end. Jesus is prepared to move on. They all knew that this would be a bittersweet parting. Eli seemed to speak for the entire group as they gathered to say farewell. "We cannot bear to have you leave us, Master. We beseech you, please let us come with you and serve you."

"Nay, it is not possible to come with me. You must go in the opposite direction, where you will serve me still. There is much territory to be covered, and the Good News must be spread all throughout Israel."

"But we are not learned men, Master. We must be taught by you before we can go out into the world," said Eli.

But Jesus said, "Even before I came to visit you, already all of you shepherds were steadfastly doing my Father's work. You have spoken the truth of what the angel said to you, even when others cursed you and persecuted you. Go now, and continue to proclaim the truth, and let all who have ears hear it."

Anam approached Jesus and, gesturing to the assembled shepherds, said, "Master, what will happen to these men? They have already suffered for so long. Now that you are here, must they continue to suffer?"

Jesus fixed his gaze upon Anam and said, "Many will suffer because of Me. Indeed, some will give their lives because of Me. And great will be their reward in heaven.

And then he turned to the shepherds and said, "In those times of suffering, remember the newly-born infant you adored on that night long ago, and I will come to you. Do not weep. I will not leave you alone. Your kindness wiped my tears when I was crying in the manger. Is my kindness not sufficient to wipe yours? In this world there will always be hatred and violence and suffering. But let not your hearts be troubled. Let my peace protect and comfort you."

Jesus then embraced each of the men and said, "What you saw that night in the stable in Bethlehem was the unfolding of God's plan to reconcile men to Himself. All will come to its fulfillment in God's perfect timing. It was with good reason that my Father in heaven chose a lowly stable as the place of my birth. It was to confound the wise of this world. They look to rich men and to palaces, but God is not impressed with these. Yea, I tell you this, all of the wealth and power of this world is as nothing to Him who resides in heaven. Creator of all that is, He asks only one thing of those whom He will call His children: that they may love Him without reservation, and accept the gift of His love as He freely pours it out unto them. Continue spreading the word of truth you have received. Go and light the fire of God in the hearts of men."

"Goodbye my friends. You have waited for so many years with patient faith. I now promise you a very short wait. But I will not leave you alone. I will return to you very soon."

And without further conversation he blessed them, and they watched him with great joy in their hearts as he and his disciples journeyed forth.